CLASS PETS

The Ghost of P.S. 42

FRANK ASCH

Illustrated by John Kanzler

SIMON & SCHUSTER BOOKS FOR YOUNG READERS
NEW YORK LONDON TORONTO SYDNEY SINGAPORE

SIMON & SCHUSTER BOOKS FOR YOUNG READERS
An imprint of Simon & Schuster Children's Publishing
Division
1230 Avenue of the Americas, New York, New York 10020
Text copyright © 2002 by Frank Asch
Illustrations copyright © 2002 by John Kanzler
SIMON & SCHUSTER BOOKS FOR YOUNG READERS is a
trademark of Simon & Schuster.
Book design by O'Lanso Gabbidon
The text for this book is set in Trump Mediaeval.
The illustrations for this book are rendered in Pencil.
Printed in the United States of America
2 4 6 8 10 9 7 5 3 1
CIP data for this book is available from the Library of
Congress.
ISBN 0-689-84653-3

FIRST
EDITION

To Linny Levin (1951–2000)
—F. A.

For my mother and father
—J. K.

 og

Many thanks to Nora Boekhout and her Web site
Classroom Animals and Pets at
http://www.teacherwebshelf.com/classroompets/

Chapter 1

Jake peeked his head out of the rusty tin can where he and his sister Molly had spent the afternoon napping and waiting for the sun to go down.

"It's almost dark enough to travel again," he announced, and sniffed the evening air.

The rusty tin can was nestled in a patch of weeds growing in the center of a vacant lot. Beyond the lot, with its piles of broken bricks, old TV sets, and moldy mattresses, he smelled car exhaust and somewhere down the block someone frying steak. "Do you remember our going-away party?" he asked Molly.

Molly closed her eyes and savored the memory of that night at Deli Dan's. All seven of her brothers and sisters had been there. And so had her fifty-three aunts and uncles. It was a memory full of tearful good-byes, last-minute advice, and the aroma of Italian sausage.

"Remember? How could I forget?" answered Molly. "It was the happiest, saddest night of my whole life."

"I was just thinking about what Poppa said when we left," sighed Jake. "Do you think he really meant it when he said we should come back if we can't find a good place to live?"

"Of course he meant it," said Molly. "Poppa *never* lies."

The two homesick mice were silent while the sky above the vacant lot turned from pinkish purple to deep violet.

Jake thought of his poppa and wondered what he was doing just then. Probably checking under the counter for scraps of salami, he guessed. Or maybe taking an early-evening nap.

Molly thought of her mother. She remembered her smell and the way she sometimes touched Molly's ears and said, "You have your grandmother's looks: same light brown fur, same face as round as a penny, same long even whiskers and tiny ears." Molly touched her own ears. *Too* tiny for a mouse, she thought.

Jake looked like no one else in the family. He had large, leafy ears, a potato-shaped head, and whiskers that stuck out at odd angles like pins in a pincushion. His chocolate brown fur was longer than even great Uncle Wooly's. And no one else in the family was so chubby that their belly hairs dragged the floor when they walked.

Jake pulled his head inside the tin can. "But would Momma and Poppa *really* be glad to see us? That's what I want to know."

Molly pictured Deli Dan's. There was plenty of food there, but too many mice. And new babies coming all the time. Even nearsighted, kindhearted Deli Dan was starting to notice. And that meant danger for the entire clan.

"They'd be glad, all right," said Molly. "But I think they'd be sad, too."

"Then, why are you being so *picky*?" squeaked

Jake. "We've been searching for three long days and three long nights, and you haven't liked a single place I've found for us!"

"Shhhhh! Not so loud!" cautioned Molly with a quick sniff. "There are rats in this lot. Smell them?"

Jake sniffed and lowered his voice to a whisper, "Well?"

Molly paused to look into her brother's worried eyes. "Here's how I see it," she said. "We're looking for a place to spend the rest of our lives, not just a place to hide out for a while. A place like that has to be special. It can't be just anywhere."

"That church I found us wasn't just anywhere!" said Jake. "Compared with the deli, it was a castle; no cats, no traps, and no poison!"

"And no food! What would we eat? Bibles?"

"The Sunday brunch they served in the basement wasn't so bad," said Jake. "We sure filled our bellies."

Jake felt a pang in his empty stomach as he recalled the taste of oatmeal, eggs, and burned toast with butter.

"We can't eat just once a week," said Molly. "And besides, it was drafty in there."

"Okay, forget about the church. I don't fancy myself a church mouse anyway. What about that big supermarket? It was packed with food, and we'd have the whole place to ourselves."

"Think, Jake!" said Molly. "All that food and no other mice. That could mean only one thing: *professional* exterminators!"

Jake opened his mouth to defend the supermarket. Then he closed it. "How about that nice old house near the river? The one with the odd smell and the purple shades? I kind of liked that place."

Molly shot Jake a dirty rat look.

"Momma and Poppa did not bring us up to live in a funeral parlor," she said firmly. "I'd rather stay right here in this vacant lot than live in a house full of smelly dead people!"

"Okay, Miss Fussy!" Jake nervously pulled at his whiskers as if trying to straighten them. "I've had it with trying to please you! From now on it's your turn to find us a place to live!"

"That's fine with me!" Molly pushed past her brother and looked up at the sky. A few stars were visible and a big yellow moon was starting to rise. "Come on," she said. "Let's go!"

Chapter 2

*I*n the rear of the vacant lot stood a tall wooden fence. Molly slipped under with ease, but Jake had to search around for a knothole large enough for him to squeeze through. On the other side they found themselves standing on blacktop beside a swing set. Next to the swing set was a slide and a set of monkey bars.

"What kind of weird stuff is this?" wondered Jake out loud.

Molly sniffed the base of the monkey bars. "Smells like kid sweat." She sniffed again. "Kid sweat, chewing gum, and soda pop."

"And what's that?" Jake pointed toward an old brick building with large windows and white trim.

"Kind of big to be a house," said Molly. "Maybe it's a store?"

The letters and numbers above the front door read: P.S. 42.

"Can you read that?" asked Jake.

Molly had taught herself how to read a few labels by watching Deli Dan unpack cartons of food in the basement.

"All I see is a *P* and an *S*," she replied after some careful thought. "The *P* could mean *pickles, pork,* or *popcorn*. And the *S* could stand for *soup, sauerkraut,*

or *sandwiches*. But I have no idea what those numbers are all about."

"I love popcorn," said Jake. "I say we go inside and check this place out."

At the corner of P.S. 42 Molly found a crack in the cement block foundation. The crack was just a little larger than her head.

"Never go where your whiskers aren't welcome," said Jake, quoting their poppa.

"My whiskers fit fine," replied Molly. "It's the rest of me I'm worried about."

"Here, let me give you a push," said Jake, and he shoved his sister through the crack.

Once inside, Molly called out, "It's nice and warm in here. I think I'm in some kind of kitchen."

"Smells good to me!" squeaked Jake. "How's the rat situation?"

Molly sniffed and sniffed again.

"No scent of rats whatsoever!" she reported.

"Good, I'll be right there!" said Jake, and he stuck his nose into the crack.

Molly waited for a full minute before she grew impatient. "What's taking so long?" she called through the crack. "I want to go exploring."

"I can't fit," confessed Jake after his third try.

"Do you want me to come out?" offered Molly.

"No, don't bother," grumbled Jake. "I'll find some other way in and meet you on the inside."

"Oh, Jake, do be careful," warned Molly.

"That goes double for you, Sis," replied Jake.

Chapter 3

It was very dark. Almost pitch black. But Molly's large eyes gathered up what little light there was like a telescope lens. What she saw was a neat kitchen with shiny pots and pans, clean counters, and not a toothpick out of place.

I like living in a clean kitchen, thought Molly, forgetting that any kitchen where she lived would not be considered clean. Molly looked all around, but she couldn't find a single crumb on the floor. Even the crackers in the pantry were kept in tightly covered metal tins.

Jake will not like this, she thought.

At the end of the hall was a staircase. Hopping from step to step, Molly climbed to the top. Then she turned and went down another hall. The first door she came to had a sign beside it that read, MISS CLARK'S CLASS.

Molly stood in the doorway and sniffed. So many new smells! For a full minute she stood there trying to sort them out. She knew the smell of kids and liked it very much. She also recognized the smell of paper, pencils, and perfume. But she had never smelled poster paint, rubber cement, or crayons before.

"Can't be a store. Hardly anything looks new,"

she said out loud. "And this place doesn't have the feel of a warehouse. So, what is it?"

Molly entered the classroom slowly, looking and sniffing up and down and all around. "Traps aren't always baited with food," Momma's words came back to her. "Sometimes clever people just leave them lying about hoping to catch one of us walking in the dark."

Miss Clark's classroom was filled with chairs and desks and lots of bright-colored paintings on the walls. Papier-mâché fish hung from the ceiling. There were maps and jars and bins and books and all kinds of places for a mouse to hide.

I think I like this place, thought Molly. *I think I like it a lot!*

Just then the big, round clock on the wall clicked forward, and Molly jumped.

Silly me, she thought, remembering the clock on the wall at Deli Dan's that made the same noise.

Amid all the new and interesting smells in Miss Clark's classroom one smell suddenly stood out: the fragrant scent of cedar shavings. Once Molly's nose locked on to it, every other smell in the room seemed to fade. Molly followed the smell until she found herself standing under a table with a sign that read, PET TABLE.

Drawn by the strong cedar smell, she hopped first to a nearby chair. Then she leaped up to the tabletop. Directly in front of her was a cage of thin metal bars. On the floor of the cage was a thick layer of cedar shavings. Squeezing her nose between the bars, Molly closed her eyes and inhaled deeply.

"Ahhh!" she sighed, and the sweet-smelling cedar filled her mind with images of cool mountain streams and deep green forests.

Tied to the bars of the cage was an upside-down glass bottle with a plastic tube sticking out one end.

How curious, thought Molly.

On the opposite side of the cage was a small pink dish full of seeds.

"Now, there's some good food!" said Molly out loud. "Looks like they built this cage around it to keep animals out."

In the center of the cage was a large white coffee cup lying on its side. Suddenly a large, tailless "mouse" walked out of the cup and turned toward Molly.

"You've got it all wrong," said the large mouse. "This cage is meant to keep animals *in* not *out.*"

The strange old mouse had a warm voice and friendly brown eyes that seemed to twinkle. He didn't smell mean or dangerous, the way nasty rats sometimes did. But something about him gave Molly a chill. Then she sniffed again and understood why: He had no odor, no scent whatsoever!

"What kind of mouse are you?" she asked, stepping back from the cage.

"Allow me to introduce myself," said the mysterious stranger. "My name is Gino. Like you, I'm a rodent. But I'm not a mouse. I'm a hamster."

Molly didn't know what a rodent was. And the only ham she had ever seen was the ham they sold at Deli Dan's.

Still feeling a bit wary, Molly asked, "What hap-

pened to your tail? Did it get chopped off in a trap?"

"Heavens, no!" chuckled Gino. "What an amusing thought. No, no! Hamsters aren't born with long tails like mice. Just little short ones." Gino turned and wiggled his tiny tail.

It looked so funny Molly had to smile, but she wasn't sure what to say next. Gino was strange. There was no doubt in her mind about that. But she saw no reason to run away. After all, he was locked behind bars.

"I was wondering what sort of place this is," she said. "At first I thought it might be a warehouse. But I can see now it's not. It smells a lot like people. But there's nobody here. I can't figure it out."

"P.S. Forty-two is a school," said Gino. "The P stands for public. The S for school. During the day it's full of kids and teachers. At night everyone goes home except for us class pets. We're the only ones who really live here."

"School? Class pets?" said Molly. "I never . . ."

"All in good time, my dear," said the kindly old hamster. "Here, allow me to show you around."

Gino started walking toward Molly with a gait so light and airy he seemed almost to float. Then something very strange happened. When Gino came to the bars of his cage, he didn't stop. He walked right through them as if they were made of mist!

Now Molly felt more than a chill. She was shocked as surely as if she had stuck her tail in a wall socket.

"Oh, I forgot to tell you," said Gino. "I'm a ghost."

Chapter 4

Jake's face hurt.

Pulling it out of the crack, he sat back and rubbed it with his paws.

"Molly would pick a place I don't fit!" Jake grumbled.

He knew he was considered chubby, even fat. All his brothers and sisters, except Molly, teased him about it. They called him Blubber Ball and Fat Buns. But Jake thought of himself as big boned and *stout*. In his mind his round belly and thick thighs had nothing to do with the fact that he ate too much and rarely got any exercise. It was a sign of his superior strength. His brawn.

When his face felt better, Jake stood up and wondered which way to go. To his right was a sea of black asphalt and the brick wall of the school. To his left was the same.

I guess it doesn't matter which way I go, he thought, and went to his right.

As he walked along, Jake looked for more cracks in the school foundation. He found a few, but they were hairline cracks, even smaller than the one Molly had found.

At the corner of P.S. 42 he came upon a metal pipe. The pipe came out of the asphalt, turned, and entered the school about two feet above the ground.

"Always check around pipes when you're trying to break into a place," he remembered his poppa telling him. Jake inspected around the pipe carefully, but it entered the school cleanly. Even a flea would have to look for another place to squeeze in.

Around the corner Jake looked up and saw a window that was ajar. Near the open window was a scraggy juniper bush. *Maybe I could jump from the bush to the window,* he thought.

Enjoying its earthy scent, Jake climbed up into the shrub. What a nose trip! He breathed deep. In all his days living at Deli Dan's, nothing had made him feel so *natural* and *wild.*

I wish I lived where there were more trees than buildings, he thought, never imagining such places really existed.

When he reached the top of the juniper bush, Jake changed his mind about jumping to the open window. The distance was just too great. He knew he'd never make it. *If only I could fly like Supermouse,* he thought.

Jake had once seen a Supermouse cartoon. But he didn't know it was just a cartoon. Not only did he think Supermice really existed, he imagined that someday he could become one. Why not? Didn't Poppa always say, "Anything is possible!"?

Every once in a while Jake checked to see if his superpowers were starting to kick in. He did this now by stretching out his front paws and waiting to be lifted to the open window. He waited and waited.

When nothing happened, he just sighed, "Oh, well . . . not yet," and carefully climbed down to the ground.

Beyond the shrubs lay the front steps of P.S. 42.

Maybe this isn't going to be so difficult after all, he thought. *Maybe I can just slip under the front door.*

Still thinking about trees and Supermouse, Jake hopped up the front steps one step at a time.

On the top step his nose suddenly warned him of danger.

CAT! CAT! CAT! his brain pulsed like a smoke alarm.

Then he saw it. A gigantic cat with gray fur long enough to be braided lay curled up on the welcome mat.

"Holy Havarti!" squeaked Jake.

Jake knew he had made a big mistake. He should have kept silent and slowly turned around. But the cat had caught him completely off guard.

One of the cat's eyelids popped up like a piece of toast. Then the other joined it.

Jake did not wait around to see what the cat did next. He jumped off the steps, rolled three times on the blacktop, and shot around the corner, looking for shelter. Jake was overweight, but he could run like a cheetah when he had to.

"You're lucky I was sound asleep," hissed the cat. "Or you'd be mouse meat by now."

Jake made no attempt to reply. He just kept putting one paw in front of the other. More than anything, he needed cover. But all around him there was nothing but blacktop and no place to hide!

Then he saw the maple tree. He knew climbing a tree to escape a cat was pure madness. But there was nowhere else to go. He leaped onto the trunk of the tree and shot upward like a rocket.

Chapter 5

"**Y**ou look like you've never seen a ghost before," said Gino.

"Well, actually, I . . . I . . . I haven't," squeaked Molly.

"There's no need to be afraid," said Gino. "Just take a deep breath and give yourself a moment to get used to the idea. I have to admit, I'm still getting used to it myself."

Molly's heart was still racing, but she could sense it beginning to slow down.

"Have you been dead for a long time?" she asked.

"I died last spring of old age," said Gino with a sigh. "Ahhh . . . seems like only yesterday I was a youngster like you. When you're young, life stretches out like an endless ball of yarn. Then one day you realize it all went by in the blink of an eye!"

Gino meant to blink. But instead of closing one eye he briefly disappeared all of himself *except* for one eye.

"On Tuesday I was playing with the kids as usual. On Wednesday they found me in my cage as stiff as a board." Gino paused for a moment to honor the memory of his own death, and Molly lowered her head out of respect.

"That afternoon Miss Clark and the kids gave me a *terrific* funeral. I was no longer in my body, so I got to watch everything. I just hovered in the air like an invisible eye. First they put me in a shoe box and taped a tissue paper wreath on top that said, 'Rest in peace, our dear Gino.'"

Gino paused again. This time a little ghost tear formed under one of his eyes.

"Then they took me outside and dug a hole near the juniper shrub right outside the window. One by one they took a spoonful of dirt and dropped it on my coffin. Then they talked about all the good things they remembered about me. I knew they liked me. But I had no idea how much. There wasn't a dry eye on the playground. Even Miss Clark cried."

Gino sighed and continued with his tale. "When they came back from my funeral, they drew pictures of me and tacked them on the bulletin board. Then they continued to talk about me, remembering more good times we had spent together. It was all *so* beautiful! But I was getting ready to say good-bye and head for hamster heaven when something quite unexpected happened."

Now Gino had two tears, one under each eye.

"One of Miss Clark's students asked what new class pet would live in my cage and all the other students shouted her down."

"No one can ever replace Gino!" they cried.

"Is that when you decided to stick around?" asked Molly.

"I just couldn't leave," sighed Gino as he wiped tears from his cheeks.

Gino was hardly more than a stranger to Molly, but she was deeply touched by his story.

"Can Miss Clark's students see you like I can?" asked Molly.

"No," replied Gino. "But they sense my presence. I sit with them when they're upset and sometimes I whisper answers in their ears when Miss Clark calls on them. And . . ."

"We see you!" came a squawk from another cage.

Only now did Molly notice the other cages on the pet table.

The squawk had come from a tall cage made of curved bamboo painted green. Most of the cage was covered with a thin blue cloth. But where the cloth parted, Molly could see four glowing eyes and the dim outlines of two beautiful birds.

Chapter 6

The gray cat walked calmly over to the old maple tree and sat down. "Who said mice don't grow on trees?" he purred.

Up in the maple Jake jumped like a sparking hot wire from branch to branch. When he paused to look down, he saw the cat beneath him purring and flexing his claws. Just like Deli Dan sharpening his knife before cutting into a side of beef, he thought.

Except for a few scattered leaves, the tree offered almost no place to hide.

When Jake ran out of big branches, he climbed onto smaller ones. After a while he ran out of those and climbed onto twigs. Only then did he feel safe enough to stop and catch his breath.

Below him the cat sat on his haunches, swishing his tail back and forth like a metronome. *If I were Supermouse, I'd grab that cat by his hairy tail and fling him over the roof tops!* thought Jake.

Then Jake remembered something his poppa once said: "When chased by a cat, always try to engage him in conversation. At the very least it will buy you some time to think. It doesn't matter what you say. Just keep him talking."

"Hrumh," Jake cleared his throat, then called down to the cat, "My name's Jake. What's yours?"

"Big Gray's my name," hissed the cat. "But don't

try to get chummy with me! I may like to play with my food, but I never make friends with it. And don't think for a moment you can lose yourself up there. I used to climb this tree when I was a kitten. I know it like I know the lick of my own mother's tongue."

"I bet your mother couldn't lick a lollipop," said Jake.

"Many a mouse has tried that old trick on me," replied Big Gray. "Don't waste your breath."

"What trick are you talking about?"

"Insulting me so I'll lose my temper," said the cat. "An angry cat is a careless cat."

"I should have known that old trick wouldn't work on a *cool* cat like you," replied Jake.

"And don't waste your time trying to flatter me either," said the cat.

"You seem to have lots of advice about what I shouldn't do. Any advice about what I should do?" asked Jake.

"That's a new one," meowed the sinister cat. "I never had a victim ask that before. . . ."

Victim, am I? Well, we'll just see about that! thought Jake.

"I always get my mouse. That's a fact." Big Gray droned on as if he were reciting a speech. "Right now you're sitting up in a tree. But soon you'll be sitting in my belly. So why mar the last few moments of your tiny life with huge, unmouselike fears?"

Poppa was right when he said cats are weird, thought Jake.

"Why not show me what a brave little mouse

you can be! Come down now and I'll gobble you up so fast I promise you won't feel a thing."

This cat has been listening to too many TV commercials, thought Jake. *Next he'll be telling me to act now while the offer lasts.*

"So come down now while I'm still in a good mood," said Big Gray. "Hopping into my mouth will be just like hopping into a cozy nest after a long, hard day. What could be better than that?"

"Are you quite finished?" said Jake. "That last part about the cozy nest made me sleepy."

"Yes, I think I've covered the main points," said Big Gray.

"Good," said Jake. "Now I've got some advice for you!"

"Is that so?" Big Gray forced a smile. "And what might that be?"

"Why don't you just come up here and get me?" said Jake. "That's what I would do if I were you."

"Ha! I might have known you would suggest something like that," snickered Big Gray. "Your motives are so simple even a kitten too young to open its eyes could see through them."

"Am I really that easy to figure out?" asked Jake.

"I'm afraid so," said Big Gray. "You want me to follow you out onto one of those tiny branches because you're hoping I'll fall and break my neck. Isn't it so?"

"Well . . . I have to admit, the idea did cross my mind," said Jake. Actually, Jake wanted Big Gray to stay on the ground. He figured that as long as he was up in the tree and Big Gray was on the ground, he was safe. "Besides, I doubt you could climb a ladder if it was lying flat on the ground," Jake added just to confuse the cat a little more.

"Still trying to make me angry, eh?" said Big Gray.

Jake breathed a sigh of relief. Some clever talking had bought him a little extra time.

Then Jake heard the hoot of an owl, "Whooo! Whooo!"

And the night sky above P.S. 42 filled with the muffled sound of wingbeats.

Chapter 7

"**Y**ou're not ghosts too, are you?" asked Molly as she drew nearer.

"Oh, no!" twittered the handsome bird, called Prince. "We're lovebirds."

"Lovebirds who are very much in love," added his mate, Princess.

"Very pleased to meet you," said Molly, and Gino introduced everyone by name.

"The pleasure is all mine," said Prince with a low bow.

"And mine, too," chirped Princess.

Even if they were called something else, Molly would have thought Prince and Princess looked regal. A matched pair, they had light green and melon-colored feathers. Their gemlike eyes were dark blue and their beaks bright yellow. The plump-chested Prince stood proud and tall upon his perch. Princess was sleek and shapely, with a long neck and beautifully curved head.

"Molly's looking for a new home," said Gino.

"Then, you've come to the right place!" said Princess. "Pets are very well cared for here. Every day the children take turns tending to our needs. They make sure our water is fresh, our newspaper is changed, and we have plenty of seeds to eat."

"That's right," agreed Prince. "Other birds must

fly about gathering food and making nests. But we have all day just to love each other."

"All day long to sing and coo," crooned Princess. "Every day is Valentine's Day for us!"

Princess looked into Prince's eyes and he stared back. For a long moment they gazed at each other, sighing as their breasts heaved. Finally Prince broke away.

"That's why our love is so deep," he chirped.

"And true!" added Princess.

Molly had never met such a pair. Even Momma and Poppa, who loved each other very much, never acted like this.

"Nothing else matters to us but our love," said Princess.

"It flows between us like honey poured back and forth between two love cups," said Prince, and once again the two birds locked eyes.

"Hruumh!" Gino cleared his throat. "I don't think either of you two quite understands. Molly's not likely to become a class pet. If she decides to live here, she'll have to keep out of sight and fend for herself."

"That's right," said Molly. "People don't like mice. They're always trying to kill us with traps and poison. I've seen them hug dogs and kiss cats with my own eyes. But when they see us, they either scream or try to hit us with a broom!"

A wave of shock spread over Princess's calm face, and two tiny feathers stood up on the back of her head.

"Why, that's just ghastly! I can hardly believe it! There must be some mistake. People are so kind," she chattered.

"Don't feel bad on my account," said Molly. "I'm used to it. And besides, I might not like living in a cage. I mean, isn't it hard for you two? Never being able to fly?"

"Oh, yes!" chirped Princess. "Before Gino died, sometimes my wings positively ached for flight."

"Mine too," agreed Prince. "Being locked up in a cage all day made us so disagreeable we ended up having quarrels."

"Lover's quarrels," explained Princess.

"That reminds me," said Gino. "Would you two like to get out tonight?"

Prince turned to Princess. "Well, dearest, what do you think? Shall we fly the night fantastic?"

Princess brushed her beak against Prince's strong neck.

"You know me, dear," cooed Princess. "I'm always ready to soar with you!"

"Very well, then," said Gino. He floated over to the lovebirds' cage, pushed back the blue cloth, and reached for the bamboo door.

As soon as their cage door swung wide, Prince hopped down to a lower perch.

Then he turned to Princess. "Ready, my dear?"

"Come fly with me!" she chirped with a laughlike twitter, and bounded through the open door. In one smooth motion she unfurled her wings and soared into the classroom.

Prince followed close behind, stopping to perch in the doorway of their cage. Looking up at his mate, he swooned, "Isn't she gorgeous? Her every wingbeat makes my heart throb!"

Then he, too, was airborne.

Soon the two of them were cutting graceful figure eights above the children's desks, swooping and diving wing tip to wing tip.

Molly had seen birds fly before, but never anything like this. Prince and Princess weren't just flying. They were dancing in the air.

"Aren't they beautiful," said Gino. "I could watch them all night."

Sometimes the couple flew so close together it seemed like there was only one bird in the air. Then they'd separate and soar in opposite directions. Prince would fly toward the blackboard, while Princess sailed to the back of the room. Then they'd turn and fly at each other. To Molly it looked like they would surely collide. But at the last possible moment Prince would peel off in one direction and Princess would veer to the other.

"Oh, look," called Prince. "The janitor left a window open. Shall we take our love flight to the stars?"

"How romantic!" crooned Princess as she flew by the open window. "But there's a chill in the air tonight. And I think I hear an owl approaching. Let's fly in the gym instead."

"Any place we fly together is heaven to me," said Prince, and the two very-much-in-love birds cut a quick turn toward the open classroom door.

Chapter 8

An ancient barn owl glided through the playground and swooped low before landing on the top bar of the jungle gym.

"Double catnip!" cursed Big Gray under his breath. "It's that old Hooter again!"

"Friend of yours?" Jake called down to Big Gray.

"Shhh!" Big Gray hushed Jake. "Be quiet and don't move a muscle. And just pray that old bird doesn't see you. If he does, you'll be airborne before you can say tuna fish!"

The old owl tucked his wings and shifted his weight from foot to foot.

"Warm night," he called to Big Gray. "Any luck yet?"

"I'm not hunting tonight," lied Big Gray. "So why don't you go steal your midnight snack from someone else? Or better yet, why don't you go crash yourself into a bus or something equally lethal?"

"You'd like that," said Hooter. "Then you could pick through my dead feathers with the other scavengers that live in this town."

Big Gray was insulted. "I'll have you know I eat only fresh meat," he howled. "But lately it seems like every time I corner a victim, you show up and steal it away."

"Oh, come off it!" cackled the old bird. "You eat more Kitty Bits than fresh meat. I've looked through your window and seen the old lady who owns you. Your squeaky cat toys and your fluffy pink pillow are no secret to me! And I've heard the clink of your dinner as it's poured from a bag into a bowl with your name on it. Now, let's see . . . what was that name? Oh, yes! Now I remember. Freddy! Isn't that so, *Freddy*?"

For a long moment Big Gray just sat there and glowered up at Hooter. "Now, you listen to me, you old feather duster! You mention that name once more, and next spring I'll find your nest and drink your babies while they're still growing in their shells!"

"No need to get your cat gut in a bundle," soothed Hooter. "I only stopped to rest. In a moment I'll be on my way."

"Humph!" grumbled Big Gray. "You only stopped to see if there was anything you could steal from me!"

"I guess I just can't stand to watch you hunt," said Hooter. "We all need to eat. But the way you torture your prey is shameless. If you were a tad smaller, I'd take *you* home for dinner."

"Just try it, and I'll scatter your feathers from here to the police station," snarled Big Gray.

"Just joking, just joking," soothed Hooter with a cackle that sounded more like a crow's call than any sound an owl could make. "No hard feelings?"

"No hard feelings," hissed Big Gray, though he obviously didn't mean it.

Then the old owl leaned forward, let himself fall, and spread his wings. As if he were a bubble blown by the wind, Hooter lifted into the air and gracefully cleared the rooftop of P.S. 42.

Watching him glide into the night, Jake thought, *That's how I want to fly. Just like that!*

"I guess this little cat-and-mouse game of ours is over," hissed Big Gray when Hooter was no longer in sight. "Now that I know that old thief is hanging around, I have to come up and get you!"

"Oh! I wouldn't do that if I were you," said Jake. "You were right before when you guessed I was trying to trick you. These tiny branches won't support your weight. Come up here, and you'll only fall and hurt yourself."

"How touching of you to worry about me," sneered Big Gray, and he leaped onto the trunk of the maple tree.

Big Gray was a very large cat, but he moved with the slippery speed of a black snake. In no time at all he reached the branch just below Jake's.

"I wouldn't come any farther if I were you. You're not the agile little kitten you once were."

"Maybe not. But I still like to play," said Big Gray.

Big Gray raised a paw and batted Jake's branch as if it were a ball of yarn.

Jake had not bargained for this. He held on with all his might. But Big Gray kept hitting the branch harder and harder.

"I haven't had this much fun in a long while," chortled Big Gray.

Then he drew back and walloped Jake's branch. Jake braced himself, but the blow was too swift and hard. It knocked Jake off the branch and sent him flying toward the ground.

Chapter 9

"What's a gym?" asked Molly.

"A big room where the kids exercise and play games," answered Gino.

"I think I passed the gym on the way here," recalled Molly. "Does it smell sweaty?"

"That's the place," said Gino. "Prince and Princess will fly fancy loop-the-loops and double figure eights in there. Then they'll fly up and down the halls and in and out of classrooms for a while. When they've had enough of that, they'll come back here and I'll let them back in their cage. Which reminds me."

Gino floated over to the largest cage on the pet table.

"Hey, Peaches, wake up!" he called through chicken wire stretched over a handmade wooden frame.

Except for something in the shadows that looked like a large ball of cotton, Molly thought the cage was empty. Then the puffy cotton ball began to move. Slowly, hop by hop, a downy white rabbit emerged from the shadows.

"I wasn't sleeping, Gino. I was listening," said Peaches. Then she turned to Molly. "And who might you be?"

"My name is Molly," squeaked Molly politely.

Peaches wiggled her nose. "That's a pretty-sounding name."

Peaches' fur looked so soft and her voice sounded so warm and inviting, Molly felt a sudden urge to curl up and fall asleep between her paws.

"I thought you might like to go out for a little hop tonight, Peaches," said Gino.

"Thanks. But no thanks," replied the large rabbit. "Tonight's my night to listen to classical music on the radio."

Molly looked around. The pet table was cluttered with smaller cages and several glass jars. Inside the jars were crickets, crayfish, snails, and one large toad. There was also an aquarium on the table with several different kinds of fish swimming in it. But Molly saw no radio, either on the table or anywhere near it.

"Pardon me," she said politely, "but I don't see a radio. And I don't hear any music."

"Oh!" Peaches wobbled her nose in a way that Molly understood to be a smile. "The radio I'm listening to is in the house across the street from the school."

"Peaches is one of the best *listeners* I know," explained Gino.

"I would be too if I had terrific ears like that!" said Molly. "Mine are kind of small, even for a mouse."

"No one should feel bad about having small ears," said Peaches. "It's small minds they should regret. Close your eyes and I'll show you what I mean."

Molly hesitated. "You want me to . . ."

"That's right, dearie," said Peaches. "Close your eyes."

"Okay," said Molly, and she lowered her eyelids.

"Now I'll point your pretty little ears in the right

direction," said Peaches. "Lift your chin up. Good! Now, turn your head slowly to the left."

Molly turned her head until Peaches said, "Stop right there!"

That part was easy.

"Now let your thoughts quiet down," said Peaches.

That was not so easy.

"I don't know how to do that," said Molly. "My thoughts are always going like flies buzzing around a lightbulb."

"What a horrid image!" exclaimed Peaches. "Let it go and try this instead. Think about something soothing, like the sound of summer rain on a tin roof. Go ahead. Try it."

Molly liked that suggestion. Lying in her nest under the pickle barrel in the deli and listening to the sound of rain on the roof was one of her favorite things to do.

"Notice how soft and comfortable it makes you feel?" asked Peaches.

Molly smiled.

"Good," whispered Peaches. "Now, listen. Really listen!"

Molly felt silly.

"I'm sorry," she told Peaches. "I don't hear anything."

"Don't give up yet," replied Peaches. "Keep your eyes closed and stay in your pickle barrel."

Molly's eyes opened wide. "Pickle barrel? I never told you about that!"

"No, but I heard your thoughts. It's not difficult

when you know how," said Peaches. "Now close your eyes."

How extraordinary! thought Molly, and she closed her eyes a second time. "The flies are buzzing again," she said.

"That's okay," said Peaches. "Go back to the sound of the rain."

Molly sighed and pictured herself back in the deli listening to the rain. She knew she was only pretending, but it made her feel safe and cozy. Then somewhere in between the sound of individual raindrops she heard a faint thread of music. It was a thin tingle of sound at first. As delicate as a spider's web. She listened some more, and the sound grew louder and clearer.

"Yes! I do hear music," exclaimed Molly. "And what beautiful music it is!"

"It's my favorite composer, Mozart," said Peaches.

"Funny you should mention Mozart!" said Gino. "Just the other day I met his pet mynah bird. Too bad none of his owner's talent rubbed off on that squawky ghost! I thought he was a nice enough chap until he insisted on singing me *his* latest musical composition. Not only did his song sound like a chorus of tone-deaf crickets, but it went on and on forever!"

Molly didn't really hear what Gino said. She was too busy listening to Mozart. After a while she said, "Now I see what you mean, Peaches. It takes more than big ears to hear well."

Again Peaches smiled with her nose. And this time Molly smiled back with her nose.

Given half a chance, Peaches and I could become fast friends, thought Molly.

34

"I taught myself how to listen when I lived on a farm," said Peaches. "Then I became a magician's rabbit. He's the one who taught me how to read minds. He did it as a trick. But I learned how to do it for real."

Just then the lovebirds flew through the open door. Dipping their wings low, they swooped down the center of the classroom straight to their cage.

"You're impossible! Just impossible!" declared Princess as she flew to her perch.

"But it's true!" insisted Prince.

"No! It's not!" squawked Princess.

The lovebirds' feathers were ruffled, and the looks that shot between them seemed more like angry spears than cupid's arrows.

They don't sound so lovey-dovey anymore, thought Molly. *I wonder what happened in the gym!*

"But it is true!" insisted Prince as he landed beside his mate. "I love you more than you could ever love me!"

"No, you don't," argued Princess. "I love you more. Much, much more!"

Prince looked pained, as if someone were trying to pluck out his feathers one by one.

"But how can that be, when you are my whole world?" he pleaded. "I love you more than fish love the sea!"

"Ha!" chortled Princess, edging away from Prince. "That's nothing compared with my love. I love you more than the sky loves its stars. You are the light of my life!"

Prince moved in close again.

"And I love you more than flowers love rain," he cooed with a gentle peck on his mate's neck. "Without you I would wither and shrivel into dust!"

"And I love you both," said Gino as he closed and locked their door. "But it's time to cover your cage again."

Soon the lovebirds were quietly cooing under the blue cloth.

And Peaches went back to Mozart.

"Now that you've met the Doves and Peaches, perhaps you'd like to see the rest of Miss Clark's classroom?" offered Gino.

"Oh, yes," said Molly. "I'd like that very much!"

Chapter 10

Big Gray did not wait to watch Jake fall. He turned and jumped down, pushing off one limb and then another, landing softly on the blacktop. He expected to find Jake sprawled out on the asphalt, stunned from the fall. But Jake wasn't there. The cat spun around. There was no hint of mouse scurrying off into the night. No sign of mouse at all! How could he have gotten away so quickly?

Big Gray was confused. He looked up into the tree. But Jake was nowhere to be seen. How could it be? Big Gray had seen him fall with his own eyes! Mice had gotten away from Big Gray before. But never had one so completely vanished into thin air!

Shaking his head from side to side, Big Gray slunk into the shadows, grumbling, "I'll find that mouse if it takes all night!"

Jake had fallen only a few feet into a robin's nest. The nest was lined with soft down. For a moment he just lay on his back smelling the lingering scent of baby robins and enjoyed the fact that he was still alive.

Now, what would Supermouse do in a situation like this? he wondered.

Slowly Jake stood up, pushed back a leaf, and looked over the rim of the nest.

No cat in sight, he thought. *But my talented*

friend could be waiting for me anywhere down there, lurking in the darkness.

Just then Jake's eyes happened to stray upward, and he noticed that the top branches of the maple almost touched the roof of P.S. 42.

Why didn't I see that before? he thought. *With one lucky jump I could make it to the roof.*

Checking to make sure he wasn't being watched from below by Big Gray or from above by Hooter, Jake slowly edged himself out of the nest and started climbing upward.

His plan seemed like a good one until he reached the branches that *almost* touched the roof. From the nest the distance between them and the roof had not seemed so great. But now he wasn't so sure. And the tiny twig his paws clung to gave him almost nothing to push off of.

Jake was about to return to the nest, when a puff of wind set the branch he stood on bobbing up and down.

That's it! he thought. *I'll get this tree to fling me onto the roof!*

Shifting his weight down, Jake coaxed the branch to dip low. Then he rose up as the branch bounced back. Every time the branch dipped low, he sank down. Every time it rose, he lifted.

It's working! thought Jake.

Jake used all his strength to swing the branch in an ever widening arc, higher and higher. Then, on an upswing, he opened his paws and let go.

Like a rock in a catapult, the branch flung him toward the school. For one brief moment it felt like he wasn't just jumping. He was flying!

"Up, up, and away!" he cried.

Chapter 11

"There's so much for you to see I hardly know where to begin." Gino lifted off the pet table and glided across the room toward one of the bookcases.

"Hey, wait for me," cried Molly. "I can't fly like that."

When Molly finally arrived at the bookcase, Gino was sitting on an open book.

"One nice thing about living here is that you'll always have lots of books to read," said Gino.

"Nice for you. But I can't read more than a few words," replied Molly.

Suddenly Gino's expression went blank and a small pinpoint of blue light appeared in the middle of his forehead.

Molly got scared. "What's that light, Gino? Is something wrong?"

For a long moment Gino just stood and stared. Then, slowly, the eerie light dimmed and vanished.

"What happened?" asked Molly. "Are you okay?"

Gino shivered and shook his head from side to side.

"Yes, I'm fine," he replied. "I just had a knowing, that's all."

"A knowing?" asked Molly. "What's that?"

"It's when all of a sudden you just *know* something," replied Gino. "I used to have knowings when I was alive, too. Only now they're much stronger and more vivid. Sometimes they come as pictures. Sometimes as words. And sometimes I just *know*. This knowing was about you. "

Molly was fascinated. "You saw a picture of me?"

"That's right," said Gino. "I saw you, as clear as I see you now. Only, it was sometime in the future."

"What was I doing?" asked Molly.

"It was very strange," answered Gino. "You were wearing tiny glasses on your nose and reading a large book."

"Glasses?"

"That's right, glasses," replied Gino.

"How can that be? Mice don't wear glasses," said Molly.

"Perhaps the glasses were merely symbolic," explained Gino. "But I definitely got the message that in the future you will read many books and become a very well-educated mouse. What I saw was that someday you are destined to become a rodent scholar!"

"I don't believe it!" said Molly. "Lots of us mice at the deli learned how to read a few words. But I could never read a whole book! Not if my life depended on it!"

"Not now," said Gino. "But someday you will. And I saw something else, too. I saw you playing with one of the kids in Miss Clark's class. It looked like you had become a class pet."

"Now, that's *really* crazy," said Molly. "Me? A class pet? I wouldn't call *that* a knowing."

Gino sighed and scratched his head.

"Doesn't seem likely, does it? But that's what I saw. Perhaps it was more than chance that led you here tonight, Molly. Perhaps it's your fate to become a class pet."

Molly was willing to accept Gino's mysterious way of knowing. Sometimes she had little knowings herself. But these particular knowings seemed utterly absurd.

"First of all," she began, "why would a mouse want to read a book?"

"Miss Clark says a book is a magical thing, like a rainbow or a drop of dew. She says a book is a spaceship, a time machine, and a best friend all rolled into one," replied Gino. "But I think they're just plain interesting."

Gino got up and looked down at the open page he was standing on. "Take this book, for example. It's called *Your Mouse.*" Gino began to read from *Your Mouse:* 'The house mouse, *Mus musculus,* is one of the most successful animal species on the face of the earth. Every village, town, and city has mice living within its dwellings, underground, or in grain stores, warehouses, and factories. If left to breed unchecked, house mice would soon outweigh our entire planet," Gino stopped reading. "Now, isn't that interesting?"

"Yes, it's *very* interesting," said Molly. "But I'm just a mouse. My brain isn't big enough to read a whole book!"

Suddenly the twinkle in Gino's eyes vanished and his face grew long. "Never sell yourself short, Molly! Never say 'just a mouse'!"

Molly lowered her gaze. Only her poppa had ever spoken so sternly to her.

But the twinkle in Gino's eyes quickly returned.

"Never mind about all that." Gino smiled. "Time will tell if my knowing was true or not. Here, let me show you something else."

Soon Gino and Molly were standing on Miss Clark's desk beside a globe of Earth.

"Know what this is?" asked Gino.

"It looks like something I once saw some teenagers bouncing in the deli," replied Molly.

"That was probably a basketball," said Gino. "Basketballs and globes are the same shape, but that's where they part company. To begin with, a basketball bounces and a globe spins." Gino spun the globe with his paw.

"I think it's prettier, too," said Molly.

"Much prettier," agreed Gino.

Suddenly Gino stopped the globe and pointed to a spot in North America. "That's where we live."

Molly looked puzzled. "What did you say?" she asked.

"I said, that's where we live," answered Gino. "Allow me to explain. The globe is a map. But it's round because we really live on a round ball called Earth."

Molly looked at Gino as if he had just said her nose was really a pumpkin. For the longest time Molly's world had been no bigger than Deli Dan's. Then she had realized that Deli Dan's was on a street. And the street was in a city. But she couldn't imagine anything bigger than that.

"Never mind," said Gino. "I'll explain all that later. Right now I want to show you"—Gino disappeared and an instant later reappeared on the opposite side of the classroom, standing beside an odd-shaped box—"this!"

It took Molly a full two minutes to make her way across the classroom to where Gino was standing.

On the way she thought of Jake.

What's taking him so long? she wondered. *I hope he's okay.*

Chapter 12

Jake landed in the gutter with a *splat!*

"Ah-choo!" he sneezed, and climbed onto the roof.

Jake shook himself and licked tiny bits of rotten leaves from his fur. Then he looked up and saw a red brick chimney sitting atop the roof of P.S. 42.

"That's it!" he said out loud. "I'll get in that way."

The roof was not steep for a surefooted mouse. But Jake had a way of stumbling over himself that could hardly be called surefooted. The more he thought about falling, the more he fell, once he even tripped over his own tail.

Concentration, he told himself. *That's what we Supermice have that ordinary mice lack.*

When Jake reached the ridge of the roof, he paused and looked down. He had never viewed the city from so high up before. All his life he had seen the world from a mouse's point of view—about an inch from the ground. Now the sight of brightly lit windows, streetlamps, and car lights stretching out to the horizon bedazzled him. *Why, that's even prettier than the Christmas lights Deli Dan hangs in the front window!* he thought.

Not too many blocks from P.S. 42 was a grassy park with lots of trees and a pond. And just look at all that greenery! Jake inhaled deeply. Even from so far away he caught a good whiff of leaves and bark. *What a smell treat!* he thought. *If I lived there, I'd make my home in a tree. Then I could smell leaves and bark every day!*

Jake looked up and saw the night sky. It was fall. The clouds had cleared, the air was crisp, and the stars flickered like millions of tiny candles. "Wow!" gasped Jake. "I bet everyone, not just mice, feels small when they look up at a sky like this."

As Jake leaned back to take in the whole view, his mind drifted like a spaceship wandering from star to star. *This world is so huge,* he thought. *I wonder how it all got started. Was there some great mouse that made it all happen a long long time ago? Or did it all just pop out of nowhere by itself?*

Jake had never had such thoughts before. Just holding them in his mind was a thrill. All he wanted to do at that moment was lie on his back and think. But his fur was still wet from the gutter and the night air had a chill. Soon he began to shiver.

Jake stood up and walked the ridge of the roof to the red brick chimney. Then he climbed brick by brick till he reached the top. Looking down into the chimney, he thought, *This will be easy. All I have to do is crawl down and I'm in!*

Suddenly Jake heard the muffled throb of wings feathering the night air above his head.

"Holy Swiss! It's Hooter!" he cried, and dropped to his belly.

Hooter's talons raked the hairs on Jake's back as a powerful swoosh of air knocked him off the chimney.

Rolling himself in his tail, Jake tumbled down the

roof until he landed with a splash in the gutter.

"Sorry about that!" hooted the old owl as he turned to make a second pass. "You should be dead by now. But don't worry. Next time I won't miss!"

Hooter was proud of his ability to attack and kill his prey in less time than it took to say, "Watch out!"

"If it's all the same to you," squeaked Jake, "I'd like to live to a ripe old age."

Jake climbed out of the gutter and scrambled up the roof. But halfway to the top he stopped. Hooter had landed on the chimney.

"Just stay calm. This will only take a moment," said Hooter. "If I do my job right, you won't feel a thing."

Leaning forward, the old hunter spread his wings and launched himself off the chimney.

Jake squeezed his eyes shut.

No amount of ducking would save him this time. There was nowhere to run. Nowhere to hide.

"Okay, superpowers," he said out loud. "It's now or never! Either you lift me into the sky or he does!"

Wings outstretched, Hooter glided down the rooftop. As if crosshairs were etched on his eyeballs, the old bird's gaze locked onto Jake. Legs lowered. Talons extended. Everything was ready for a success-ful kill.

As the critical moment approached, however, a gush of air rising from the roof created an updraft under Hooter's broad wings. Hooter instantly low-ered his tail feathers to compensate, but the updraft was too strong. The sudden breeze lifted Hooter right over Jake's head.

"Blasted wind!" cursed the old bird.

Jake looked up, surprised to find himself still there.

"What superluck!" he cried.

Now Hooter would have to fly in a big circle to make a third pass. That gave Jake just enough time to scramble up the roof, climb the chimney, and jump!

"Ooow! Ooow! Ooow!" Jake bounced off the inside of the chimney until he hit the bottom with a thud.

"Ooof!" Jake landed on his back, knocking all the air from his lungs.

Surrounded by a thick blanket of total darkness, Jake stood up and checked for broken bones. There were none. But every muscle felt sore and bruised.

Where am I? he wondered. *Sure is warm in here!*

Jake sniffed.

Smells like soot. Soot and . . .

There was a *click* sound, and a tiny blue flame ignited a few inches from Jake's face.

That's better, he thought. *At least now I can see.*

Then there was a hiss and a noxious smell filled the air.

Suddenly a row of gas jets under Jake's feet burst into flame.

"Oh, Lordy Limburger!" he cried. "I'm in a furnace!"

Jake jumped back from the hot flames. He had no idea where an escape exit might be or even if there was one. He just kept hopping from one row of gas jets to the next, always just one hop ahead of the spreading inferno.

The heat was scorching. It dried Jake's fur, curled

his whiskers, and singed his eyebrows! When he reached the far end of the furnace, there was nowhere left to jump.

Jake's thoughts spun like a pinwheel: *How stupid of me to die like this! No one will even find my body. I'll be cremated! I hope Molly has better luck. Too bad I didn't get to live in a tree. I would have liked that. So, these are my last thoughts. Hmmmmmmm . . . not very interesting . . . oh, well . . .*

Jake took one last breath and prepared to die. But in that breath he smelled fresh air.

He looked up and saw a round air vent just above his head.

Flames shooting up all around him, Jake stepped back and jumped!

Chapter 13

"**I** know what this is," said Molly, proud to know something for a change. "It's a computer. Deli Dan uses one to pay his bills."

"That's right," said Gino, pushing the Power button. "But have you ever been on the Internet?"

Gino's paws danced over the keyboard.

"What are you doing?" asked Molly.

"Entering my password," replied Gino. The computer clicked and whirred as Gino typed, "* * * * * * ."

"You wouldn't know to look at it, but this little box has thousands and thousands of books inside it," said Gino.

Gosh, those books must be very tiny, thought Molly.

"Want to help me work the mouse?" asked Gino.

Molly looked in the direction Gino was pointing, but she didn't see anything that looked like a mouse.

"What mouse?" she asked. "I don't see a mouse."

"You're standing right next to it," said Gino.

Beside Molly was a curved gray box just about her size.

"That?" she exclaimed.

"Yes, that," said Gino.

"Is it a robot mouse?" she asked, wondering if the wire connecting it to the computer was some kind of tail. Then she sniffed the box, wondering if there was a real mouse inside.

"Don't be afraid," chuckled Gino. "It doesn't bite. Just give the mouse a shove and notice how the little arrow moves on the screen."

Molly did as Gino said. Pretty soon she was moving and clicking the mouse as if she had done so all her life.

"You're a natural," said Gino. "Now, tell me something you've always wanted to know more about."

Molly thought for a moment. "One day I heard Deli Dan say the moon was made of green cheese. I've always wondered how big it is."

"Okay," said Gino. "Let's type in 'moon' and see what we get."

Soon a photo of the moon flashed on the screen.

"That's what the moon looks like up close," said Gino. "Now let's see what it says: 'The moon is Earth's only satellite. It is 238,857 miles from the Earth, which means that if you were to drive there in a car at seventy miles an hour, it would take you one hundred forty-two days to get there. It measures 2,160 miles across and weighs eighty-one quintillion tons.'"

"Wow!" said Molly. "That sure is a lot of cheese!"

After looking up *moon*, Molly wanted to know about meteorites. Pretty soon she and Gino were surfing the Net, going from topic to topic. After *meteorite* they looked up *satellite*, and after that *space program*. Molly was amazed to find out that the very first astronauts from Earth were mice.

"So we were first in outer space," said Molly. "I don't think even Poppa knew that!"

"I actually met that mouse," said Gino. "Nice fellow. Of course, he's a ghost now, but he still loves outer space. Spends most of his time on the new space station."

Molly couldn't get enough of Web surfing. But Gino wanted to show her some games. Molly's favorite game was Shape Up.

"I love making those little squares line up," she told Gino. "I wouldn't be surprised if it was a mouse that invented this game."

"We could look that up," said Gino. "Or I could show you something else."

"There's more?" asked Molly.

"Of course," said Gino, and he clicked a box marked E-MAIL.

"It gets pretty lonely around here at night sometimes, so I taught myself how to use E-mail. Since then I've been sending and receiving E-mail messages from all over the world. I just have to be careful and erase them all so Miss Clark doesn't find out."

Gino had six messages in his mailbox. One was from a scientist who worked at the Bronx Zoo researching hamsters. He had no idea he was really talking with a hamster ghost. Another was from a parrot in Japan who sent messages by pecking at the keys.

"And here's a message from a hamster friend of mine inviting me to his deathday party," said Gino.

"Deathday party?" asked Molly. "What's that?"

"It's like a birthday party," answered Gino. "Only

instead of celebrating the day you were born, you celebrate the day you died. Every year you light another candle on your deathday cake and give away presents to all your friends. It's great fun, really."

Having a ghost for a friend is going to take some getting used to, thought Molly.

"I won't answer these messages now," said Gino. "I thought you might want to go shopping."

"Shopping? Where?" asked Molly.

"On the Internet," answered Gino.

"You mean you can buy things with this box?"

"That's right," said Gino. "How about your very own book? Or maybe you would prefer a big wheel of cheddar cheese? I could have either delivered to this classroom by tomorrow afternoon."

Molly never got to make that choice because just then a strange black mouse appeared at the doorway.

Chapter 14

Molly had seen mice with black fur before, but never one that looked so absolutely jet black from nose to tail. Every part of this mouse, its feet and nose and ears, was the exact same shade of black. *Maybe it's not a real mouse at all,* thought Molly. *Maybe it's some kind of ghost I don't know about yet!*

The black mouse, trailing tiny black footprints, walked into the classroom, sniffed the air and squeaked, "Hey, Molly, it's me—Jake! Are you in here?"

"Rye bread and crackers! It's my brother!" Molly squeaked so loud she nearly woke up the lovebirds. "Jake! Jake! I'm over here! Over here!"

Jake looked up and grinned. "Oh, mouse! Am I glad to see you!"

Molly felt a rush of sisterly love. What a joy it was to see her brother's chubby form, his big ears and crooked face.

"What's the black for?" she giggled with relief. "Some kind of Halloween costume?"

"That's not funny," fumed Jake. "I fell into a furnace and nearly burned to a crisp."

Molly suppressed her giggle. "Are you okay, then?"

"Yeah, I'm okay," grumbled Jake.

"Then, come on up here," said Molly. "I want you to meet Gino."

"Meet who?" Jake squinted and looked confused.

"I don't think he can see me," said Gino. "Not many can."

"Never mind . . . just come on up," said Molly. "I'll explain when you get here."

Jake and Molly had lots of catching up to do.

"You'll never believe all the hassle I had getting into this place," he said. "First I ran into this cat called Big Gray, and then . . ."

Molly listened to every word of Jake's adventure, all the while wondering how she was going to break the news about Gino.

How would I react if the tables were turned? she asked herself. *Would I believe in Gino if I couldn't see him?*

Finally Jake finished his saga. "So that's it," he said. "Now, tell me what happened to you."

"Well . . ." Molly began by describing her journey from the school basement to Miss Clark's classroom. Compared with Jake's action-packed yarn, her tale was boring. Boring, that is, until she got to the part about Gino.

"Oh, come on, now!" said Jake. "What really happened then?"

"I told you," said Molly. "Then Gino walked through the bars of his cage and told me he was a ghost!"

"Molly, have you eaten anything strange lately?" he asked, looking closely at her eyes.

"What has that got to do with anything?" snapped

Molly. "And stop looking at me that way! I'm not crazy. I really did see a ghost. In fact, he's right here now!"

"Sure he is," said Jake. "And I'm a dog."

Molly sat back and gave Jake a hard look. "Are you calling me a liar?"

"All I'm saying is you must have eaten a moldy bean or something," replied Jake. "Why else would you be seeing things?"

"I haven't eaten anything since yesterday when we shared that piece of stale bread," said Molly, and she gave Jake a moment to let that sink in. "I know this is hard to believe. But there really is a ghost that lives in this school."

Just then Gino decided to shut down the computer. He pushed a few keys. The computer made some whirs and clicks, and its screen went blank.

Jake jumped back. "What was that? Who turned the TV off?"

"It's not a TV," said Molly. "It's a computer. And it was Gino who turned it off."

Jake took another hard look at his sister. "You're not kidding me, are you? You really think this place is haunted!"

"I never said it was *haunted*," replied Molly. "I said there was a ghost that lives here. That's all. Haunted is something bad. Gino's a good ghost."

Jake scrinched up his eyebrows and tugged on his whiskers.

"Ooookaaay," he said. "So where is this *good* ghost? Hiding in the walls or something?"

"He's standing right beside you," said Molly.

Jake stiffened.

"If you're making this up, please stop," said Jake. "I'm not in the mood for practical jokes tonight. Really!"

"I'll try touching him," said Gino. "Maybe that will help."

Gino reached out and nudged Jake's shoulder with his nose.

"Yikes!" Jake jumped straight into the air. "Something just touched me!"

"I know," said Molly. "It was Gino."

"Well, tell him not to do it again!" insisted Jake.

"Does that mean you're convinced?"

"Convinced enough to want to leave right now," said Jake. "I'd rather live in two funeral parlors than a haunted house!"

"It's not *haunted*!" insisted Molly. "It's not even a house. It's a school. And I like it here. I like it here very much."

Jake could hardly believe what he was hearing. "You, Miss Fussy, want to live in a haunted school with a kitchen that's cleaner than a raindrop? Err . . . maybe I should go out and try coming back in again."

Molly was ready for a fight. "First of all, don't call me Miss Fussy, and second of all—"

"Wait a minute," interrupted Gino. "You two aren't getting anywhere, and I've been a poor host. Why don't you both take a break and have something to eat. You must be starved. Molly, bring your brother over to my cage and I'll share some of my old hamster food with the both of you."

"Well?" said Jake. "Why are you so quiet? Is the ghost talking to you?"

"As a matter of fact, he was," said Molly. "He wants to feed us."

"Food?" said Jake, forgetting everything else.

"That's right," said Molly, and she led Jake over to the pet table.

When they reached Gino's cage, Jake's gaze went straight to the pink plate of seeds. He wasn't sure he wanted to eat "ghost" food, but his growling stomach was not in a fussy mood. He put his nose between the bars and sniffed.

"Gosh, that smells good," he sighed.

Suddenly several seeds in Gino's food dish rose up into the air.

The seeds seemed to float all by themselves across the empty cage. Then they passed through the cage bars and came to rest in a neat pile in front of Jake's paws.

"Wow!" said Jake. "There really is a ghost in here!"

"I told you," said Molly as she picked up a pumpkin seed and popped it into her mouth.

"Wait a minute," said Jake. "Maybe you shouldn't eat that."

"Why not?" said Molly.

"If it's from a ghost, it could be poison," replied Jake.

"Gino's a friend!" said Molly, and she picked up another seed.

Jake stepped forward and sniffed at the pile of seeds.

"Smells okay," he said. Then he picked up a sunflower seed and turned it around in his paws, inspecting it from every angle.

"For mouse's sake, Jake! It's not a haunted seed," said Molly. "Eat it!"

After a brief struggle Jake's caution gave way to his hunger. "Here goes," he said, and took a tiny nibble.

"Mmmmmmmm . . . not bad," he reported after a few chews. "Not bad at all."

Somehow Gino knew that food was just the right thing to change Jake and Molly's mood.

When the pile of seeds on the pet table dwindled, Gino went back in his cage and got some more. While they ate, Molly told Jake all about Gino, Peaches, and the lovebirds.

When their stomachs were full, Jake and Molly felt much better.

"Now to clean that soot off your brother's fur," said Gino, and he opened the door to his cage. "The water from my water bottle will be just the thing."

Jake, like most mice, preferred to be neat and clean whenever possible, but he was reluctant to go inside Gino's cage.

"What if he wants to trap us in there?" he whispered in Molly's tiny ear.

"There's no point in whispering," said Molly as she walked into Gino's cage. "He's standing right beside you."

Jake stood by the open door trying to make up his mind.

"Well," said Molly. "Do you want to clean your fur or not?"

How come I never feel like Supermouse when I'm around Molly? Jake wondered to himself, and he walked into the cage.

"Just have him touch the nozzle like this," said Gino as he showed Molly how to use the upside-down water bottle.

Then Molly showed Jake.

"Not a bad gizmo," said Jake as his chocolate brown fur slowly emerged from the sooty black. "You say your ghost lived his whole life inside this cage?"

"His name is Gino," corrected Molly.

"Gino, Beano, whatever," said Jake. "It seems like a rather dreary existence to me."

"I'm not suggesting we live in a cage," said Molly. "We can build nests in the walls. In the daytime there are people here. But at night we'd have the whole place to ourselves."

"And what would we eat?" asked Jake. "Gino's seeds were excellent. But one plate of food is not a food supply! And what would we drink? We'd need water, too."

"Tell Jake that there's a leaky pipe in the basement where you can always get fresh water," said Gino. "The kids always leave unfinished sandwiches and treats in their desks. And there's lots of seeds, beans, and macaroni from art projects that end up on the floor."

"Say, what's that mist in the air?" asked Jake, pointing toward Gino.

"That's me," said Gino.

"Oh, my!" Jake's jaw dropped. "The *mist* just talked to me."

"That's no mist," said Molly, jumping up and down with excitement. "That's Gino!"

"Doesn't look like much to me," said Jake. "In fact, it's fading."

"Keep looking," said Gino.

"Did you hear that?" asked Molly.

"Hear what?" replied Jake.

"Quiet your mind and concentrate," said Molly, remembering what Peaches had told her about listening. "Think of something peaceful, like rain on the roof."

"That's silly," said Jake.

"Just try it!" insisted Molly.

"Okay," said Jake, but he didn't think of rain on the roof. He thought of trees. Lush green trees waving in the breeze. And it worked. Instead of fading, the mist thickened. Slowly it churned like milk drops in water and began to settle into a definite shape.

"Yes, I think I see him now," said Jake. "At least, I see a furry blob."

"Keep looking!" said Gino.

"I heard that. I heard it loud and clear this time," said Jake. The furry blob slowly took on more specific form. Soon Jake saw the body and face of a scruffy old hamster.

"So, you're Gino," he said at last.

"Pleased to meet you," replied Gino with a wink.

"I always thought seeing a ghost would be scary," said Jake. "But I'm not afraid at all."

"Not now, maybe," said Molly. "But you were at first."

"Was not," said Jake.

"Were too!" said Molly.

"Was not!" said Jake.

"How about you?" Molly asked Gino. "Were you scared when you saw your first ghost?"

"Come to think of it"—Gino paused to search his memory—"I never saw a ghost until I died and looked in the mirror."

"That must have been kind of scary," said Jake.

"As a matter of fact, it was," replied Gino. "Say, are you two sure you've had enough to eat?"

"I'm stuffed," said Jake with a loud burp.

"Me too," said Molly. "How about you, Gino? Do ghosts ever get hungry?"

"I don't eat earthly food anymore," answered Gino. "But I do partake of a light snack when I visit hamster heaven from time to time."

Suddenly there was a loud *clunk!* from across the room. They all turned to look at the same time. A hairy gray beast had jumped up from the ground and was now squeezing through the open window.

"Run for your lives!" cried Jake. "It's Big Gray!"

Chapter 15

Big Gray's gaze went straight to Jake.

"So, we meet again," he said, jumping from the windowsill to the floor. "What a delicious pleasure!"

"The pleasure is all yours!" replied Jake.

"Yes! Very soon." Big Gray grinned a huge Cheshire cat grin that made him look like an old mop with teeth. "First, I want to know how you got away. I saw you fall. Then you disappeared. How did you do it?"

"Sorry, it's a trade secret," answered Jake, and he thought: *We Supermice never reveal our methods.*

"No matter. I've found you again. That's what counts." A loud purr erupted from Big Gray's throat. "I was starting to feel lonely without you. I looked everywhere, high and low. I even passed up other mice along the way. You know how it is when you have a craving. When you have to have that *certain something* and nothing else will do? That's how I feel about you!"

"How flattering," said Jake. Then he whispered to Molly, "He looks fat and clumsy, but don't be fooled. He's *very* fast."

"I heard that!" snarled Big Gray. "And I am very fast. Amazingly so! But most of all, right now I'm hungry. So hungry I could eat a three-course meal.

You'll be my appetizer." He nodded toward Jake. "Then I'll have the big one for my main course." He looked straight at Gino. "And you, little squeak," he spit at Molly. "I'll save *you* for dessert!"

"So, he sees me," said Gino. "That's good. *Very* good!"

"It is? Why?" asked Molly.

"You'll see," said Gino, and he disappeared into thin air like a soap bubble.

"Where did he go?" cried Jake.

"I'm over here," called Gino from the computer table. "Just keep your friend busy while I call in some backup."

Just then Big Gray leaped from the floor to the pet table, slamming into Peaches' cage.

All this time Peaches had been quietly listening to her music program. Her thoughts were with Mozart. But Big Gray crashing into her cage got her full attention.

Sizing up Big Gray at a glance, she quipped, "Look what the cat dragged in—himself!"

"Mind your own business, Cotton Ball!" hissed Big Gray. "Or I'll come in there and chew your ears off."

"I wouldn't try that if I were you!" Peaches thumped the bottom of her cage like an air hammer.

Big Gray did not want to tangle with Peaches. "I've got tonight's menu all planned out," he said. "And you're not on the menu!"

As Big Gray straightened up he backed into the lovebirds' cage and knocked their blue cloth to the ground.

The two birds made a charming sight. Each was

standing on one foot, leaning against the other as they slept.

Prince was the first to wake.

Looking straight into Big Gray's face, he chirped, "Shhhhhhh! Don't make a sound. You'll wake up my mate!"

Big Gray made a loud caterwaul. "Wake your mate! Ha! I'll do more than that! I'll eat your mate and you, too!"

Just then Princess woke with a start.

"Oh, my!" she chirped. "I'm having a nightmare. I'm dreaming I see a horrid cat outside our cage!"

"No, my sweet," said Prince. "You're not dreaming. That *is* a horrid cat outside our cage!"

Big Gray began to drool. If there was one thing he loved more than mice, it was birds.

"So, you're *sweet,* are you?" said Big Gray. "Normally I don't eat sweets. But in your case I could make an exception."

Suddenly Molly found herself jumping between Big Gray and the lovebirds.

"You leave Prince and Princess alone!" she cried.

Molly had just made a foolish move and she knew it. She knew she ought to run. Run now and run fast. But she couldn't help herself. She couldn't stand by and do nothing while that miserable cat threatened the Love Birds.

"My, my," said Big Gray. "What a brave dessert we have tonight."

"Get back! Molly! Get back!" cried Jake. "We've got to scram!"

"Appetizer is right!" said Big Gray. "But it's too late now!" And he sprang into the air, straight toward Molly.

Chapter 16

"**M**issed me!" cried Molly, and she jumped off the pet table onto the floor.

"Not for long!" howled Big Gray. "Here I come!"

Now it was Jake's turn to play hero.

"Hold it!" Jake boldly strode forth. "Aren't you going to eat your appetizer first?"

In his mind Jake was dressed in blue tights. A red cape flapped behind him in an imaginary breeze. He stood upright and inhaled deeply, puffing out the big *S* for Supermouse that was emblazoned on his chest of solid steel.

"What?" Big Gray was caught off guard. In all his years of mousing he had never encountered a foolhardy pair such as Molly and Jake.

"I said, aren't you going to eat your appetizer first?"

"Don't worry"—Big Gray let Molly go and turned toward Jake—"I won't forget you. I promise!"

"Promises, promises," mocked Jake. "You've been making promises all night, but you haven't kept a single one!"

"Oh, yeah?" Big Gray's sinister purr grew louder. "We'll see about that."

While Jake kept Big Gray busy, Molly made her way across the classroom to where Gino was tapping on the keyboard of Miss Clark's computer.

"Just what do you think you're doing?" asked Molly.

"Contacting the OWW," replied Gino.

"OWW?"

"Other World Web," said Gino. "There. I got it!"

Suddenly the image of a bright blue sky and clouds flashed onto the screen.

Then Gino typed, "deadpetsociety.com."

"I don't understand," said Molly. "Jake is . . ."

"I'm contacting the Dead Pet Society. All dead pets get free membership the day they die. It's a great organization with loads of benefits and lots of useful services. Now, let's see. . . ."

Gino typed "Dog" in a small box. Beside it he wrote, "Mean looking." Then he pushed the Return key.

A little ghost image turned around and around for a few seconds. Then photos of several mean-looking dogs appeared on the screen. There were bulldogs with big teeth hanging over fat lips. There were German shepherds with heavy brows, pit bulls, and ferocious-looking rottweilers.

"I really don't think this is a good time to be Web surfing," said Molly.

"Which dog looks the meanest to you?" asked Gino.

"Gino, I don't think you understand our situation," began Molly. "You're already dead, but we—"

"But I do understand, Molly," replied Gino. "And I'm trying to help. I think the pit bull looks ferocious.

But the German shepherd may be bigger. What do you think?"

"I think we have to do something about that cat before he eats my brother!" cried Molly.

"Never mind," said Gino, and he typed: "SOS. Need help now!" Then he clicked twice on the picture of a German shepherd with a heavy brow and gigantic teeth.

Immediately a large bark came from the computer. It was so loud it hurt Molly's ears.

"Stand back!" cried Gino. "He's coming through!"

No sooner had Gino spoken than big black paws and legs burst forth from the screen. Then there was another bark, and the dog itself followed, jumping out of the computer and onto the classroom floor!

Chapter 17

"**W**ho needs help here?" barked the gigantic canine.

At last Molly understood what Gino was up to.

"We do," she cried. "A monster cat is attacking us!"

Gino double-clicked on the square marked BIO.

"Says here your name is Helmet and you died in a fire."

"That's right," replied Helmet. "I was playing with my master's little girl when a fire broke out in the house. I managed to pull her from the flames. She survived, but I died of smoke inhalation."

"Did it hurt a lot?" asked Gino.

"Oh, not much," said the canine ghost as he let his snarl go slack. "What got you?"

At that moment Jake was racing across the class-room floor with Big Gray just inches behind.

"I hate to be pushy," said Molly, "but my brother is about to be eaten by a cat. Could you two ghosts discuss your deaths some other time?"

"Of course!" growled Helmet, summoning the wicked snarl back to his lips. "Just point me at that nasty cat, and I'll scare the daylights out of it!"

"Over there! By the oak desk!" cried Molly.

"I see him!" woofed Helmet, and he leaped toward the desk.

Helmet overtook Big Gray with a few quick

strides. Then he turned and faced him.

Big Gray put on the brakes and slid to a stop just inches from Helmet's paws.

With legs spread and head lowered, Helmet said the one thing that cats never ignore: "Grrrrrrr!"

"Catnip!" howled Big Gray. "Who let you in here?"

The hair on Big Gray's back stood up so straight he looked like a porcupine.

"I let myself in!" snarled Helmet, and he took a step forward. "I let myself in, and now *you* will let yourself out!"

"I just came in here to eat some mice." Big Gray's tone was cool, but his eyes twitched with malice. "You dogs say you're man's best friend, but humanity hates mice. Shouldn't you want me to kill and eat as many loathsome mice as possible?"

Helmet took another step forward, and Big Gray took a step back.

"These mice happen to be friends of a friend," said Helmet. "If you know what's good for you, you'll leave them alone."

"Whatever you say, big guy," answered Big Gray.

Realizing that the tables had turned, Jake stepped forward and stood between Helmet's legs.

"That's right, Freddy," said Jake. "This is your appetizer talking, so pay attention! From now on you'll be a good kitty and stay home! Stay home, eat your Kitty Bits, and lick your fur all day! Got it?"

"Don't count on it!" mumbled Big Gray.

Jake's gaze shot up toward Helmet. "Did you hear that?" he squeaked.

"I'll tell you what I'm going to do," said Helmet,

and he took another step forward. "I'm going to shut my eyes and count to three. When I open them, I expect to see you gone. And I never want to see you again! Is *that* understood?"

Big Gray looked up and nodded.

"Good," said Helmet, and he closed his eyes and started counting. "One . . . two . . ."

When Helmet reached three, he opened his eyes expecting to see Big Gray's backside as he ran for his life. Instead he was confronted with Big Gray's stare. Big Gray had not moved an inch. Helmet knitted his huge brow.

"I changed my mind, Pooch!" snarled Big Gray. "I decided that you're not what you seem to be."

Helmet was caught off guard. "Is that so?" was all he managed to say.

"That's right," said Big Gray. "Just before you closed your eyes, I looked into them. And you know what?"

"No, what?" growled Helmet.

"Your eyes are not the eyes of a killer. You wouldn't kill a flea. Not even a mean one. You're a pushover. That's what you are. A baby, a certified puppy dog. You don't have a mean atom in your body. You only *look* mean!"

Helmet swallowed and his snarl went slack a second time. He hadn't had a cat turn on him like this since he was a puppy. And the worst part was, Big Gray was right. Helmet *didn't* have a mean atom in his body. Actually, since he was a ghost, he didn't have any atoms at all!

Big Gray took a step forward, and Helmet took a

step back, which left Jake standing out in the open.

"Uhh . . . errr . . . I think I have some other things to do right now," Jake chattered nervously. "So if you two don't mind, I'll be going. . . ."

Jake lurched forward, but Big Gray had other plans. With one quick motion he reached out and slammed his paw down onto Jake's tail. Jake tried to run, but his paws just spun on the linoleum like car wheels stuck in deep snow.

"Let the mouse go," demanded Helmet. "Let him go or—"

"Or what?" hissed Big Gray.

Chapter 18

Molly was almost hysterical.

"Please, Gino!" she pleaded. "Do something! Do something quick!"

"What can I do?" said Gino. "I'm just a hamster. No, not even a hamster anymore. I'm just a ghost!"

"What!" Molly's eyes lit up like road flares. "How can you say that? Weren't you the one who hit the roof when I said 'just a mouse'?"

Gino paused for a moment.

"Okay! I get the point!" he said, and disappeared.

"Gino! Where did you go?" cried Molly.

Then Molly looked down and saw Gino on the floor facing Big Gray.

Big Gray blinked. "Oh, look! It's my main course. My entrée for the evening. Where'd you come from?"

"You don't want to know where I come from," said Gino in a low, threatening voice. Unfortunately, Gino's lowest, most threatening voice still sounded a lot like a hamster's squeak.

A bemused look crossed Big Gray's face.

"I just don't believe it!" he snickered. "*You* are trying to scare *me*! Am I missing something here?"

"Okay! That's it!" said Gino. "I warned you!"

"Listen here, pip-squeak . . . ," began Big Gray.

Gino took a deep breath and puffed himself up to twice his normal size.

"What the . . . " Big Gray flinched.

Gino took another deep breath and grew some more. It was like someone was pumping him up with a bicycle pump. Every time Gino breathed, he grew bigger and meaner looking.

"I'm seeing this, but . . . but I don't believe it," stammered Big Gray. "What are you? Some kind of ghoul?"

"That's right," said Gino "I'm a school ghoul. And my job is to protect this place from creeps like you!"

Gino's voice grew as deep as a bear's growl, and his front teeth sprouted into three-inch-long spikes.

Big Gray cringed, but he kept his paw on Jake's tail.

Gino took another inhalation and towered over Big Gray.

"You better scram!" said Jake. "Pretty soon he's going to be big enough to eat you!"

Big Gray looked more confused than scared.

"Wait a minute," he said, and sniffed. He sniffed Gino, and then he sniffed Helmet. "Neither of you two has any scent. Ha! Now I get it! You're not real! You're just *ghosts*! That's what you are!"

"You're not afraid of ghosts?" said Gino in his newly acquired deep monster voice.

"Heck, no!" said Big Gray. "I'm a cat. We cats are friends of witches. Nine lives and all that. See?" And with that Big Gray lifted his paw and struck out at Gino's face.

His paw cut through Gino like an airplane slicing through a cloud.

"So I was right!" said Big Gray. "You two are nothing but spooks! Mere wisps in the night!"

Jake did not stick around to see what happened next. As soon as Big Gray lifted his paw, he cried, "Got to go!" and made a desperate dash for his freedom.

He flew like a hockey puck on ice straight across the classroom floor. He didn't notice that the moon had set or that the sun's warm glow was casting pink squares of light on the blackboard. But he did catch a glimpse of Miss Clark standing in the doorway.

Chapter 19

Miss Clark was a tall, young woman with long black hair, which she wore in a ponytail. This morning she was wearing a blue skirt and a white blouse with a red poppy in her lapel. Her outfit, especially the poppy, made her look old fashioned. But she liked that look. It reminded her of her mother, who had also been a teacher.

Miss Clark had come in earlier than usual to correct some papers. As she paused before entering her room she didn't see Gino or Helmet or Molly, or even Jake. All she saw was Big Gray.

"I must remember to tell the janitor never to leave the window open at night," said Miss Clark as she picked up Big Gray and escorted him to the front door of the school.

"My, you *are* heavy," she said as she set Big Gray down on the blacktop and stroked his head once or twice. Exploring with her fingers through the thick fur around Big Gray's neck, she found his identification tag. Satisfied that Big Gray was not a stray, she stood up and said, "Now, run along home. School's no place for a house cat!"

By the time Miss Clark returned to the classroom, Helmet had already left. And Gino, having restored himself to his normal size, and shape, was showing

Jake and Molly where they could stay inside the walls of P.S. 42.

"Right this way," he said, and led them to a piece of loose molding behind one of Miss Clark's bookcases. Gino easily slipped into the wall, but Molly and Jake had to squeeze in between the molding and the wallboard.

"Just follow me," said Gino when they were both inside.

"But it's all black in here," said Jake. "How can we follow you when we can't see anything at all?"

"Or even smell you," added Molly.

"Sorry," said Gino. "How's this?" And he made himself glow with a dim greenish light.

"Now you look like a real ghost," said Jake. "How did you do that?"

"Darned if I know," said Gino. "It just happens. Same way your tail moves when you want it to."

Following Gino's ghostly trail was easy.

As they made their way through the wall Molly said, "That sure was a surprise when you turned into a monster like that. What gave you the idea?"

"It was a surprise to me, too," replied Gino. "But it didn't do much good once Big Gray guessed I was a ghost, did it?"

"It only saved my life!" exclaimed Jake.

"I don't know about that. But one thing's for sure"—Gino turned and smiled a ghostly grin at Molly—"from now on I'll never say 'just a ghost.'"

Gino led Molly and Jake on a long trail through the wall. Then he stopped and said, "Listen."

"I hear a clock," said Jake.

"Me too," said Molly. "It must be the one on the back wall."

"That's right," said Gino. "And look over here." Gino showed them where a tiny nail hole let some light into the wall. "The person who hung that clock missed the beam with the first nail. That's why I thought this spot might be a good place for you two to settle. Not only will you have some light coming through that nail hole, but you'll be able to see out into the classroom anytime you want."

"I like that!" said Molly. "This is a perfect nest site. Don't you agree, Jake?"

Peering through the tiny nail hole, Molly looked out into the classroom and saw Miss Clark at her desk.

"What a fine person," she said, and sniffed through the peephole. "Why, that's the lovely perfume I smelled when I first came in the classroom." Molly couldn't take her eyes off Miss Clark. "I don't know why, but I have the feeling I'm going to like her," she announced. "I *know* I'm going to like her a lot."

"Let me have a turn," said Jake, and Molly moved aside.

Jake looked and sniffed.

"I think she has a candy bar in her purse," was all he had to say about Miss Clark.

"I'm going to head back to my cage now," said Gino. "I want to be ready when the kids come in. We can talk later when you've had a good rest."

Then Gino simply floated through the wall.

"Wish I could do that!" said Jake.

"Me too," said Molly.

Suddenly Gino's head popped back inside the wall.

"You two are going to stay, aren't you?"

"Oh, yes!" said Molly.

"Good," said Gino. And he disappeared again.

When he was gone, Molly said, "I think we've made a good friend tonight."

Jake yawned and curled up into a ball. "It's been a long night. I'm beat!"

"Me too, but I'm not sleepy," said Molly. "I guess I'm just so excited that we finally found a place to live."

"Wait a minute," said Jake. "I never said I wanted to stay here for good. We need shelter for the daylight hours. That's all. When it gets dark, I say we move on."

"But we just told Gino we would stay!" complained Molly.

"*You* told Gino," said Jake. "Not me."

"But I like this place so much!" cried Molly. "Why, you have no idea what I learned just tonight! I tell you, Jake. The world is so much bigger and more interesting than I ever thought it was!"

"Funny you should say that," yawned Jake. "That's just what I learned tonight when I was up on the roof. It was so neat up there! I saw the whole city laid out below me like a blanket of lights. And the stars in the sky! Wow! There's just no words for it!"

"This place is good," said Molly. "We should stay."

"I saw something else up there too," said Jake. "I saw a place that was nothing but trees. Dozens and dozens and dozens of good-smelling green trees. As soon as I saw them, I thought: *'That's* where *I* want to live!'"

Molly stared at Jake in utter amazement.

"You want to give up this place, this wonderful place, with food and water and friends, to live in a tree?"

"I know it sounds crazy," said Jake. "But there's something about the smell of a tree that makes me feel so . . . so . . . different!"

Molly remembered how the smell of cedar shavings had made her feel. "I think I know what you mean," she said. "But we can't live on smell. We need food and shelter and water. And this place has *all* of that."

Jake just sighed.

"Oh, Jake, I really love this place. I can't fall asleep until you agree to stay."

"I'd rather talk about it tomorrow," replied Jake. "I'm too tired to think now."

"Please, Jake, can't you make up your mind now?" begged Molly. "This place has *everything*. We could make a real home here. Tell the truth. If you were the one who had found it, you'd be *crazy* about it!"

Jake sighed and thought for a moment. He just couldn't get the place with all the trees out of his mind.

"But what if the trees turned out to be a better place!" he said.

"And you called me fussy!" squeaked Molly. "Just

how long do you want to keep looking? A week? Ten days? A month?"

"Okay. Okay! I give up! If it makes you happy, we'll try this place out. If it works, we'll stay. Is that good enough? Can I go to sleep now?"

"Oh! Yes!" cried Molly. She was so tired and happy, tears filled her eyes. "And I hope you have the most pleasant—no, the most wonderful dreams in the whole world!"

"I doubt it," said Jake. "I'll probably dream about cats and owls and furnaces."

"And trees!" said Molly. "Don't forget trees. Oh, Jake! I'm so happy. At last we found a new home! If only Momma and Poppa could see us now. They'd be so proud of us. Aren't you happy too?"

When Jake did not reply, Molly nudged him with her nose.

"I said, aren't you happy too, Jake?" she asked again.

This time Jake replied with a snore.

"Oh, well," sighed Molly. "He must be exhausted. And I'm tired too." Molly yawned and closed her eyes. "I'll always remember this night. Our first night in our new home!"

Molly was still too excited to fall asleep right away. Scene by scene she reviewed all that had happened since she and Jake left the deli. Skipping over all those aimless days of wandering, she savored her first impressions of Gino and Peaches, and the thrill of watching the lovebirds fly. No longer just recent events, these recollections had already become fond memories.

And the last things Molly thought about before falling asleep were Miss Clark and Gino's knowing. *Poppa always said, "Anything is possible,"* she thought. *I wonder if the day will ever come when I'll be a class pet.*

And she began to dream.